TROUBLE

Also by Herbert Lomas

CHIMPANZEES ARE BLAMELESS CREATURES
Mandarin Books, 1969
WHO NEEDS MONEY?
Blond & Briggs, 1972
PRIVATE AND CONFIDENTIAL
London Magazine Editions, 1974
PUBLIC FOOTPATH
Anvil Press, 1981
TERRITORIAL SONG
London Magazine Editions, 1981
FIRE IN THE GARDEN
Oxford University Press, 1984
LETTERS IN THE DARK
Oxford University Press, 1986
CONTEMPORARY FINNISH POETRY
Bloodaxe Books, 1991

TROUBLE

Herbert Lomas

Dear Barbara — A thankyou note
and a belated birthday present
after the Champagne and
delicious fare so unexpectedly
served up to me. It was a great
evening + so nice to meet you —
Ever —
Bertie
30 September 1996

SINCLAIR-STEVENSON

First published in Great Britain
by Sinclair-Stevenson
7/8 Kendrick Mews
London SW7 3HG, England

Copyright © 1992 by Herbert Lomas

A CIP catalogue record for this book is available from the British Library.
ISBN 1 85619 1737 (hardback)
ISBN 1 85619 2016 (paperback)

Typeset by Rowland Phototypesetting Limited
Bury St Edmunds, Suffolk
Printed and bound in England
by Clays Limited, St Ives plc

For Mary

ACKNOWLEDGEMENTS

The poems have appeared in *Ambit, Encounter,*
The Hudson Review ('Chanson Triste', 'Other Life',
'First Kisses', 'Assisi and Back', 'In Spite
of Everything', 'Suffolk Evenings'),
London Magazine, New Spokes, Poetry Durham,
P. N. Review, and *The Spectator.*
My thanks to these editors.

Contents

I: FEUX D'ESPRIT

Trouble

*'I will be no trouble to you. I sleep
all day, go to the theatre in the
evening, and at night you may do
what you will with me.'*

– Marie Duplessis to Liszt

That summer's lakeside cabin makes me sigh:
that manic horse, too, with his madhouse eye –
in love with you. As was I.

As we trailed to the farm for milk, he ran like my heart
thudding across the field: nose over gate;
and once – did he vault it? – out in the night,

he'd nibbled your drawers on the line. Ass!
An edge of dissolved-in-saliva grass
greened the last shreds of your silkiness.

When I cracked a window, at your wish
I rowed and sprinkled the splinters: a dish
for the water sprite – and we never lacked for fish.

The ancient pike I caught's huge jagged
crocodile snout scowled, as it rose and wagged.
And now your hatred, even, that's almost flagged.

Greenwich Park

Spring's come, a little late, in the park:
a tree-rat smokes flat S's over the lawn.
A mallard has somehow forgotten something
it can't quite remember. Daffodils yawn,
prick their ears, push their muzzles out
for a kiss. Pansies spoof pensive
Priapus faces: Socrates or Verlaine.
A cock-pigeon is sexually harassing
a hen: pecking and poking and padding
behind her impertinently, bowing and mowing.
But when he's suddenly absent-minded
– can't keep even sex in his head –
she trembles, stops her gadding, doubts
and grazes his way. He remembers and pouts.

Chanson Triste

The leaves on the lawn under the chestnut
are suddenly shocking
like something squandered.

His aching head
will rest in summer moonlight's lap
and the poems he'll read
will make her *prima vera*
high summer and autumn all at once.

In her melancholy eyes
he'll drink so many kisses
so many caresses
he might even be cured.

Or is he drinking with so much pleasure
the old illness
through the new kisses?

A piano made out of water
and clouds
and sunlight
is taking a golden glamour
into its greyness.

For years
one can rely on
an imaginary love.

Remembering Adlestrop

I too remember Adlestrop –
that hot compatible weekend in the car
when all the birds of Gloucestershire
seemed intoxicated by tar

and dawdled on the road. I slowed
to let them loop away. 'Adlestrop
must be here, I bet,' I said.
And then, towards dusk, a sudden stop:

a signpost: 'Adlestrop!' I cried,
not really having looked, and turned.
No railway: just the station sign,
yellow, conserved; and I somehow yearned

and grieved as a blackbird sang.
Had I an inkling even then that now
I'd hear it with wringing pain,
knowing your love had stopped, not how?

Other Life

She was a burning glass.
A little sun inside had passed
through her from a hotter source.

And yet she was opaque.
Made from a childhood ache
that dark as particles could flame and shake.

She was dark, dark
and almost out of sight: a watermark
pressed in the paper of her book.

The book was all she'd been,
child, mother, slut, queen,
and all she'd ever done or seen.

If he'd read her,
he'd have learned to dread her,
certainly never dared to kiss her or bed her.

Shingle Street

Someone lying on the deserted beach
appears to be lying on someone else.
She lowers her head
and drinks him slowly,
holding him by the ears.

He's completely not-there,
and she, with her black hair
is a bee-sucker
after nectar
under his grey hair.
They must know I'm coming,
but they don't care.

It must be illicit,
nowhere else to go,
not going to be stopped
by my possible stare.

Rules are overnice
in Paradise.
Though no one marries
or gives in marriage,
their bright ice,
great seers say,
melts in the solar flare
of their fusion and confusion.
That's how they feel each other there.

Who doesn't wish them well?
Perhaps we too
in some afterlife
will find some angel
to give us fugitive love
when ordinary women no longer find us
worth the worry of.

First Kisses

The best kisses are the first.
First mother's kisses, and after that
the kisses in the Botanical Gardens
stolen among flowers.

Then there are the kisses when
you think you'll never be kissed again.

Kisses in foreign cities:
perhaps in a flat, perhaps in a rainy street,
panting because illicit.

And then, late at night, comforting
someone in tears. Perhaps it's because
she's so hot with suffering, or hasn't
used her kissing mouth for almost years.
But probably not: she just has a talent
and like so many talents, it's
been buried.

                            Like her breasts
with their talent for being looked at and
looking back, it's a hidden address.

Not for everyday visit or caress.

Assisi and Back

It's the train from London to Assisi,
a sort of pilgrimage:
in the diner a dark girl
is staring: I feel my age.

It's the train back from Assisi, and the same
dark girl, suddenly aware:
so she smiles, sits close, intensely
close, and deplores her stare.

I'd like to say, You're lovely, but
as I'm old enough to be
your daddy, a man
must keep some dignity.

But on the platform at the end I give her,
unexpectedly, a kiss.
Her friends shriek, and she
wanders off in, apparently, bliss.

It's pleasant enough
to remember her now.
'I' seem young and naive –
she showing me how.

But why was I afraid of her?
Is it cowardice? And this
convergence? Surely not
a hint from St Francis –

knowing so much more now
than under his vow,
joined properly with poor Clare
up there?

Two-hundred-mile-an-hour Winds

Sometimes a friend can disappear
completely out of the crowd:
a silver finger
points out of a cloud.

Two people and a donkey sailed away –
tornadoed – miles in air –
let down later that day,
alive, but stripped bare.

Wonders occur to every doubter,
your friend not noticing, though, or caring to:
but you don't feel right about her
after, or she you.

Refractions

We can do no great things
but only small things
with great love
says a mother in Calcutta.

An old man kneels
round his wife's grave
hedge-clipping grass:
to serve, to grieve.

A dead seagull in a flooded ditch
on a dark night
has one wing raised
as if for flight.

An elaborate lamp
reflected in the window might
make it seem
as if there were no night.

In Spite of Everything

In spite of everything, I think
mostly of you, even though
this is the century of mass death,
gas, squandering of resources,
and pollution of the future.

Though our grandchildren curse us, as they will,
limping and tottering with diseases
we dumped on them with war research and waste,
and millions are lying belly-bloated in Africa,
I think mostly of you.

Though trees are dying, I think
mostly of you, almost always, wondering
if your smile is an acid rain, or if
you really love me, and I can't have enough
of your unattainable presence and perfume.

Most of all I long to know
what you're thinking really, and this
obliterates the kneecaps blasted off in Ireland,
the profits from sophisticated weapons,
state terrorism, daggered idealism,

big dealers lobbying the government,
the investment of labour and wealth in futility,
the expense on defence on a planet
that's been indefensible ever since
the last of England were signing 'There'll always be an
                                                     England'.

Unaccompanied Voices

An imitation of
Eugenio Montale's 'Mottetti'

1

You know it: I have to lose you again
and I can't. Each act, each cry,
snipes me, and the blown salt too
swilling the harbour mole
and making the sombre spring
of Sottoripa.

Region of ironware and rigging –
a sort of forest in the dusty evening.
From out there comes a long rasping –
grating like a nail on the window.
I look for the lost sign, the single
token you graced me with.

And I'm certain of Hell.

2

Many years, one somewhat harder: an *agon*
on a foreign lake burning with sunsets.
Then you descended from the mountains,
bringing me Saint George and the Dragon.

If only I could print them on the banderole
the north-east is whipping
in my heart . . . And through you enter
a whirlpool of fidelity, immortal.

Frost on the windows; together
for ever, the sick, and for ever
apart; and, at the tables there,
the long *post-mortems* on the cards.

The exile was yours. I think again
of my own, the morning shock
of that bomb, 'the ballerina',
blasting off among the rocks.

And they dragged on, those night games,
that fiesta of artillery flares.
A brusque wing brushed and checked your hands –
but no: the card wasn't yours.

Though far away, I was close
when your father entered the shades
and gave you his goodbye.
What did I know till then? I survived
all that in the past only through this:

that I didn't know you and had to.
Today's shocks tell me – bringing back
an hour down there, Cumerlotti
or Anghebeni: the shellbursts,
the groans, and the charge of the cavalry.

Goodbyes, whistles in the dark, waving,
the coughs, and the lowered windows. Time to go.
Could be the robots are right. How they stare
from the corridors, walled in!

Does the faint litany of that intercity
make you too remember
the dreadful precise cadenza of the samba?

6

The hope of ever seeing you again
abandoned me;

and I wondered if these things that cut me off
from all sense of you, these sort of movie-shots
in the street, were symptoms of death
or past shots of you: distorted and fleeting
flashes of pastiche:

(at Modena, for instance, between the porticos,
a liveried servant dragging
two jackals on a leash).

7

The black and white swoopings of swallows
from telegraph pole to sea
are no comfort to your pierside sorrow,
will never take you where you no longer are.

Already the elder is spreading its fragrance
over the diggings: the squall is dispersing.
The clearing sky is a truce, maybe,
but your sweetness is another threat of rain.

8

Behold the sign, nervously printed
on a wall going gold:
a jagged shadow of palm-leaf
burnt there by the shine of dawn.

Dawn's gentle pace
down from the mountains
isn't muffled by snow, is still
your life, your blood in my veins.

9

Suppose a green lizard, darting
from the stubble,
under the great whip –

or a sail, fluttering out
and sinking
by the steep bluff –

the noonday cannon
fainter than your heart, and
the chronometer
striking without a sound –

and what then? It'd be vain

for a lightning flash to change you
into something rich and strange.
You were made of different stuff.

10

Why delay? In a pinetree a squirrel
is whipping his torch-tail on the bark.
A half-moon is dipping its horn
in the sun and being snuffed. Day's begun.

A gust startles the sluggish mist:
it recovers at the spot shrouding you.
Nothing will end, or everything, if you
come flashing out of the cloud.

11

The spirit that polkas
and rigadoons at every new
season of the street feeds on
locked-up passion, finds it
intensified at every corner.

Your voice is this diffused spirit.
By wire, by wind, by wing, by chance,
by favour of the muse, or some machine,
it comes back, happy or sad. Talk supervenes
with people who don't know you, but your imago
is there, singing on and on: *doh ray me fa so . . .*

12

I free your brow of the icicles
you picked up, traversing those high
nebulae; your wings are lacerated
by cyclones, you wake with a start.

Mid-day: the medlar stretches a black shadow
across the square; in the sky a chilly sun
persists; and the other shadows, slipping
round the alley corner, don't know you're here.

13

The gondola that glides in a great
glory of tar and poppy,
the sly song that rises
from masses of rigging, the high doors
locked on you, and the giggles of the masqueraders
who scamper off in swarms –

it's an evening in a thousand, and my night
is still more pregnant! I'm roused with a start
by a pale tangle writhing down there,
equating me with that rank
aficionado, eel-fishing on the bank.

14

Is it salt or hail raging furiously down? –
massacring bellflowers, uprooting verbena.
An underwater tolling
like the one you induced
is coming and going.

Hell's pianola is speeding up, reaching
higher and higher registers, by itself, climbing
the spheres of ice . . . – brilliant as you
taking off Lakmé's *Bell Aria*
with that trilling coloratura.

15

At first light, when
the sudden rumble
of an underground train tells me
of trapped men in transit
in a tunnel of stone
lit by inlets
of mixed sky and water –

at first dark, when
the woodworm that tools through
the writing-desk doubles
its fervour, and the tread
of the watchman is coming –

at first and last light those stops are still human,
if you keep threading them together.

16

The flower, repeating
from the edge of the gorge
'forget me not',
gets no sunnier or gladder tints
from the space thrown between you and me.

A screech of metal, we're lurched apart,
the steady blue won't come back.
Through an almost visible sultriness, the funicular
is taking me back to the already-dark far stage.

17

A frog, first to try his vocal chords
from the pond of mist and reeds, a sough
from the cluster of carobs where
a chilly sun is extinguishing its torches,
the slow flowerward drone of beetles
still sucking sap – the last sounds,
the greedy life of the campagna . . .
                              A breath of air
blows the hour out: a sky of slate
is getting ready for an apocalypse of bony
horses, with sparking hooves.

18

Shears, never cut that face,
that fine listening look of hers,
and make an everlasting mist
of the only image I clearly remember.

It's getting chilly . . . A hard cut:
and the pruned acacia sheds
a cicada shell
in the first mud of November.

19

The reed softly moulting
its red fan in spring;
the dragonflies hovering over
the black water running in the ditch;
and the dog panting home
with something heavy in his mouth –

today, no hint of recognition
for me here: but where the reflection
burns fiercest in the fosse
and the clouds lour, beyond her
eyes now so remote, just two
strands of light form a cross.
                    And time passes.

20

. . . Well, let be. The sound of a cornet
converses with the bees, swarming in the oaks.
On a shell, reflecting the failing light,
a painted volcano cheerfully smokes.

The coin, too, locked-fast in the lava
gleams on the table, holds down a few
loose leaves. Life that seemed so immense
is briefer than your handkerchief.

II: ESPRIT DU SOIR

We are survivors, in this age, so
theories of progress ill become us,
because we are intimately
acquainted with the costs. To
realize you are a survivor is a
shock.

> – *Herzog*, Saul Bellow

Solvitur Acris Hiems

An imitation of Horace,
ODES I iv

Stinging winter dissolves. At the sweet swing of spring
    and the west wind, dry hulls trundle to the shore,
sheep bleat at the fold, the shepherd leaves his fire,
    and the fields unfreeze their frosty white.

Venus brings the girls out dancing under a hanging moon,
    with all the Graces, pounding the earth,
and Vulcan stokes his huge blazing furnaces up,
    eager for the summer lightning.

Now it's time to oil our hair, prick ourselves out
    with tiaras of myrtle, put on flowers from the melting
                           earth.
And now's the time to remember the gods in their shady
                                groves
    and give them a lamb or goat for good luck.

Death's white face looks impartially at the pub door
    and the palace gate, O lucky Terry, and kicks at both:
the sum total of anybody's days is short, so hopes should
                                be:
    ghosts, nothing but names now, crowd round you, and
                                night,

and the thin exile of Hell. Once down there, no
    shake of dice'll make you the gracious host.
No ogling of pretty boys then, whom everybody adores now
    and the girls'll soon burn to make a pass at.

The Wild Swans at Aldeburgh

Some days they look like outsize geese
with no secret, seen
waddling across reclaimed land
to a ditch. Thirteen:
my lucky number. But one, hatched out too late,
is without a mate.

The trees are in their winter grandeur.
A line of pine trees stands
aware of me as I of them –
children holding hands.
We watch a ditch ruffle like elephant skin
and the sun whiten and thin.

I track a curlew in a cloud
by its call: fast headway.
The thirteenth swan has taken off:
an immature grey,
it creaks a low flight, then stands and walks alone,
feeling its half-soul gone.

Pathetic these fallacies our lives fatten.
Forty years are lost
since I first read Yeats, yet I never see
a swan without his ghost.
A swan in death and I in life both read
the bobbin, rewinding the thread.

December sunshine brings white joy,
a milky hole in light.
These weeks three friends or almost-friends
have taken that silver flight
to some new pond or ditch or reclaimed land.
As souls, or swans, we stand

in a place of no giving in marriage.
Aware or unaware,
a leap through inarticulate light
defines some strangled prayer,
leaving us stripped, deciduous winter trees,
hand in hand, or on our knees.

Sea Lady

Someone's crept out of the sea,
lying on the pebbles, in pain:
a crippled labrador.
She raises one arm, a lady
in a siesta, languidly,
though night's falling, and this January rain.

Hearing my crunch on the shingle,
she's turning bitch-soft eyes and whiskers to vet me.
I'm coming too close,
and she growls, hisses and whispers,
tensing my tail with her speech,
though I know she can't get me.

Hurt? Perhaps she's tired?
But I'm too close, so she levers her spine
and flops down a shingle bank, enters the ocean,
periscopes twice with her head,
then hoists ashore,
crutching her legless rear up the steep incline.

Who'd be sick, if they lived in the ocean?
And who'd bark
so hard after fish, they'd give up the earth,
lose hands and legs,
freezing the warm blood back
to the cold, to feel after fish in the dark?

I sit in my lights by the fire, listening to Mozart,
reading Gibbon.
A Diocletian legionary, an old lag
looking for loot, found
a beautiful leather purse of priceless pearls.
He threw the swag away and kept the bag.

For what's no use can have no value.
And in the morning she
who loves the waters I left behind
is gone like a piece of flotsam,
a bag of pearls,
that is and always will be far out at sea.

Suffolk Evenings

1

Evening's always a favourite time,
a lazy man's time, and autumn a favourite season,
for those who know they're living in failing light.
And failing light's internal. Sea and night
toil on but – it's more
of a vocation than a task. A ship snores
out of the scud, honking of risky work.
I turn to the fire and a different kind of dark.

An atmosphere close to pain; it implies
that all you've ever done, even your lies
and cruelties are invited: evening companions
to sit over tea or whisky and teach you sums,
equations once unteachable. Too
incalculable a calculus. On the pebbles, in a shampoo
of greening sea, bottle or log comes back in surges,
always erasing us, of selves.

To the child who still hurts me it was hard to believe
in a time of no canals: so like rivers:
no barges now, but heavy with frogspawn and duckweed.
You dive off a lock into ink. From the balustraded
balcony at the back of the house, you could see
a water-rat launch in a widening and widening V.
The navvies are all dead, and what they left is a clear
stretch of almost stillness that's always been there.

2

The tiny hands of rain on the window
rap a rainy Pennine childhood
in an eighteenth-century house
of pre-technological people: a grandma
born in the 1840s, an aunt

fifty already, my mother forty.
I crawl by the big black fireplace,
with the blackened copper kettle on the hob
that sings quietly by the flapping flame
as if we were wintered-in at Grasmere.
The huge kitchen's always dark:
lights burn by day; the only window's benighted
by the high bank glooming the yard at the back.

My dad's preparing himself a grog
in the stained-glass bar, I'm
on my farm with the lead sheep, drawing up
the drawbridge on my flagged fort,
or reading *The World's Great Books in Outline*:
pictures of Dante and Beatrice, my mother's
name, and *A Midsummer Night's Dream*:
Fuseli's vicious fairies: subfusc landscapes
with holes of light, no different from
the darkness under the table with the cat,
or the days of rain drenching the valleys,
or the watery window, where tiny hands are picking
and knocking and running down like tears.

                        3

        A ship snores out of the scud,
        honking of risky work.
        I turn to the fire
        and a different kind of dark.

        Evening: thoughts slip into night:
        the flash of a lightship
        just out of sight
        has a name I've never found out.

        A brass show dangles from my lamp –
        bought just before that
        cancer-test: a gipsy called,
        and told me I'd live to be old.

                        31

On a sunny afternoon
the door crashes open,
a guitar string snaps; the cat sees
a nothing there – screams and flees.

A man on the beach,
with a gold umbrella,
taps it like a white stick: not only
deafened but blinded by the sea.

For another the sea's his mother:
she's telling him something serious
that makes no sense, as if
she were a piano, and he the audience.

4

A white ferry strolls the horizon line:
a floating hotel, crystalline.
So much light and so much going.

Light as paper, seagulls
shriek and dip,
comparatively grey and dirty
with their angel-wings.
Sunset seeks the ship.

The other selves are creeping close tonight,
studying me: they made the choices
I didn't make. They lived promiscuously
with strangers for years and years,
becoming stranger to me,
with different wives and different lives,
taking the faces of strangers into their own.

A lightship
over the horizon,
invisible by day,
winks in evening wrack,

and, as I look,
signals knowingly back.

A ship snores out of the scud,
honking of risky work.

In the room there's an almost stillness
that's always been there
and tiny hands are picking at the window
and running down like tears.

Heron

The crematorium sits quietly by a river,
bosky, bird-haunted, willow-fringed.
At this double rendezvous,
fishing is dawdling by water
with apparently something to do.

Success is cruel: a fish flaps,
aghast at the thing in its mouth,
the net round its scales, the pain of air.
Yet a sharp smack on the back of the neck,
and the pain's not there.

The heron angles with no licence,
but glimpse a watcher, and he's off:
an awkward contraption with a glued head,
long S of neck, and a dangle of legs:
or a child playing airplane, arms spread.

In water he strides circumspectly,
not to tread on something sharp,
his knee at 90 degrees.
Feels down softly in the mud,
with his claws and his elbow-knees.

Apparently asleep or thinking,
he listens for fish. Long beak
pokes, gobbles, and his swallow
is quick. Stowed, he stands and meditates
and his flap away is slow.

Now in another place he works alone
somewhere beyond all this,
while the other watchers only wait,
scanning us from a new angle,
silently interested in our fate.

A herd of snipe are grazing:
hungry Chinamen
prodding chopsticks in a stew:
I'm absent; but once a lapwing
looked in my binoculars as if he knew.

Ashes

In memoriam Geoffrey Castle,
6 April 1898–8 February 1990

The sun's bright: it's like a shopping trip.
It's the young man's lunch hour, but the ashes wait
gravely on the desk: metallic-brown, a cheap
plastic concave-sided mini-crate,
with an oilcan screw-top and an awkward fit
of a named and numbered self-adhesive chit.

'Can you return it, please? Believe it or not,
they cost seven pounds.' About as hard to make,
I think, as a detergent bottle. Why not depute
a fruit jar? – be cheaper and less fake.
I hold it tight and, trudging to the car,
my stomach tingles, feeling he's still there.

It occupies the mantelpiece and shapes
the whole room round it. Our lady
comes to clean, sees it and escapes.
He sits there, waiting his day: martinis,
gravlax, fillet, dual-coloured mousse,
a wine. But first we let him loose.

The wind's keen from the north, grooming the coast;
a pewter sea pours oyster waves.
In the evening sun a gibbous moon due east
looks somehow prescient, unduly grave.
The ashes pass from hand to hand; we three
watch, as one in daffodil waders walks the sea.

And the ashes pour like milk or sand.
Back, his bosun's whistle pipes three times.
And do they come, stand airily close at hand?
The stage is set – for invisible mimes
or empty coulisses. It's in reverse:
we speak to the stage: they don't converse.

The world is our idea. Turning from the mind,
we crunch the pebbles. The weathervane
points north: from behind that wind
the dead supposedly come. And now the main
has a different constitution, its whitening hue
white ash, like the waning man we knew.

I asked him, if he could, to let me know.

Ignorance

I sit in the great ignorance,
in a vast church in a city of doors.
Workmen bang and boom: a restoration
beyond a bewilderment of floors.

In the nothingness where I sit
circling buses and taxies peal,
like the peel from an orange
that's eaten and once was real.

Empty space always amazes, the something
that nothing was, with wrapping moods.
And later, locked in, unnoticed, I thump
twin doors: they burst, and the lock protrudes –

a tongue, but whether for insult
or kiss, or whisper, it's difficult to say.
But tongues remind of love
and love is suffering today.

My friend is dead. The glass is broken.
Emptiness remains without its shell:
and emptiness speaks, and silence,
though neither speaks well.

Nightfears

Clambering to dark on the top-floor corridor's
row of moonlit rooms, you meet those eyes
and bony legs stalking the draughty floor.
You snatch the switch, to exorcise
the creaking boards and the paper faces
that ogle through the walls their old grimaces.

You sleep in shirt and pants, too scared
to be exposed or dowse the light.
Why was it no one cared
to tuck you in or say goodnight –
or noticed creased-up pants, the smell?
Why were you too afraid to tell?

And what to dream of in the dark? At times
you're a crew, wrecked in the arctic sea,
slipping their dinghy, to die betimes,
not linger in mist: choosing to die,
you know that moments later a ship will find
the man who chose to freeze and stayed behind.

Why this fear of the dark, this reluctance to tell?
New islands shine, new fauna and flora
emerge, mature, ripen, swell
and rot. Still at the tiller, there's Horror,
but you, strapped to the mast,
tune to blue night, coming, and coming fast.

Keith Vaughan's Last Journal

I thought last night about Boulanger, baker
of warm new bread, his own: those pearly nipples,
and that navel – another pearly acre.
Legs straight and strong, no bulging muscles.
I kissed him so many times. We had no sex.
Held him in my arms and touched his head,
breathing gently against each other's cheeks.
And six weeks later, Anzio Beachhead,
blasting to bits his lovely wine and bread.

That listening Japanese: beauty like the meat
of a wild cat: lotus lips and hawked
eyebrows; olive skin, widespread thighs, neat,
though little showing between. Stripped,
strung, slightly plump, by his wrist, naked
to a high bar, with a whip cracking, a fist
between the thighs, could I crack
the marble open of that smug conventionalist?
Ah, Boulanger, the hot bomb you kissed!

And life after death? Just guesswork. Oblivion!
Back, back to the state we had before
our birth: that beautiful death. But am I one
to do it at night? For then, happily, I snore
in my cups. Nothingness: what sleep can be –
what I itch for in the morning. But if the blood's
empty of drink, will the drug bring eternity?
I must be practical: death hardly could,
once the decision's made, be left to a mood.

The mask of Tutankamoun: the inorganic
universe of rock and water: onyx eyes,
gold, tear-stained cheeks. The kick
as it sees right through you. Childish, wise,
sad round the mouth, how understandingly
the face would make you go on trying. If God could woo

that way, I'd love his power, turn devotee.
The artificer of that mask certainly knew
and loved the godlike face that's peering through.

The camera reveres what's there: it can't
imagine the unseen. Those pursing lips
are poised to open, to receive. Eyes slant,
and – possibly – venom to spit. We strip
to meet a naked god: BC, three thousand-odd,
and yet it's Christ. He judges not. You
look at a king and he keeps looking: a god.
Even I could be happy, should I do
anything as beautiful as you.

Rock's where we come from and where we soon
go back: the kingdom of stone and water. And so:
viaticum, the capsules, the whisky, and the swoon.
How unreal, no bang, no wrists. I know
I'm dying yet feel no different. A bright
sunny morning like those so many die in.
I feel so alive. I feel no fright.
I do fear death but want it, let it come.
I might of course wake up. I did some . . .

Meeting

When I was supposed to meet you
to discuss my breakdown
the pub was full of drunken Orangemen
on their annual screw of the town.

I knew I was there on my own
but not why.
Had you put me there
to make me feel more alone?

My poems are all written to you,
even the scurrilous things:
especially the scurrilous ones –
trying to test your meanings.

You've sung to me in a pop song
and it's you who invented play.
If your cards are close to your chest,
I know you're not what they say.

Every day's a different story,
though I don't always see it as new.
I'm not always listening,
at least not always to you.

Who thinks they're unconventional?
Let them listen to you.
You're utterly outrageous.
You've seen everything through.

You saw it before it happened.
In the pub you were really there.
You know I can never be without you.
You invented the notion of dare.

Growing Up in the Thirties

1

What day of the week was it – a Sunday?
He heard his father's shout upstairs and ran,
smelling the gas. She lay on a divan,
fishmouthed, unbeautiful, a face of whey.

She's still his mother, he loves her still.
And yet her face – it's like his grandma was
in the coffin, her sharpened nose and toes
when, forbidden to peek, he did for the thrill.

Or Antarctic Scott in the white film of those
losers in blizzards, drudging from the Pole:
cut off from affluence, the dressed-for-dinner role,
they pass their dead friend's grave and icicle nose.

Outside: flies heatstroked on the burning flags,
the boy next door bouncing a ball, trying
to dot them. Now he must hide his mother's dying.
As flies to wanton boys – school-Shakespeare rags.

2

She can never pass a mirror. It feeds her greed
to know she's there, suddenly grey: a gaping beak
famished for herself. Yet Sybil, matriarch,
Rochester's wife: medium and mother in need.

Bony hands are clasping, can't stop wringing.
Legs must pace. Insufferable energy drives
the suffering machine: handwashing wives
can act the Lady Macbeth, neck-tendons stringing.

Set books at school are all about his home:
Paradise Lost, the sulphurous lake,
Rochester's secret, the visions of Blake.
Quo Vadis makes the room a burning Rome.

Out on the Rec, the click of a cricket bat,
a shout, a cheer. On the swings Harry's
doing his Harry Roy. His crooning carries:
'This is yer old watcher-me-callum', flat.

3

Ruth stood among the alien corn,
loving to play her Haydn; also bright.
Not a great looker, or the sort to bite –
that the local lads'd feel and get the horn.

He loved her in his way, perhaps because
her life was not a matter of mere survival.
Himself, he summoned Beethoven, felt the arrival
whenever he beat C minor chords.

At the Gaumont he hardly dared to touch
her hand in the flickering black and white.
Her head's rigid as a sentry's, it doesn't seem right.
Oh! fear of rejection, oh need to clutch!

In the carriage back it's so difficult to chat.
Packed close with her's enough to make him hot.
Then down the train, a shout from a drunken sot.
It's Dad again, pissed, from a night out.

4

Outside the house, the usual gang of cheerful louts –
one in particular known to have fucked a pig.
The grammar-school cap can make you look a prig.
'A chip off the old potato!' – the usual shout.

Dad knows they spoil the street and hates
the prick to his pride still more: he stalks out,
and they break into cackle, scuffling about.
The beast's on the street. It only waits.

Hard at his sums, he hears his dad brought in,
K.O.'d by the boar that's married to a sow.
Right's on that side, for Dad is snoring now,
death in his breathing, slaver on his chin.

The newsreels know the ghettoes: mugs like those
can smile and smile: now the fact of race
smashes a world of glass, or a mother's face.
So should one be a Charlie, thumb the nose?

The Long Retreat

One day in the Long Retreat they
were reading in the refectory Sister
Emmerich's account of the Agony
in the Garden and I suddenly
began to cry and sob and could
not stop.

> – Gerard Manley Hopkins,
> *Journal* 23.12.1869

Dear father, when I remembered your tears,
as I sipped some wine on a calm evening, I peered
out at my garden where a ravening blackbird
was picking for worms and a holly tree's
spikes seemed to be twisting its spines, and I
wept some tears like yours, knowing that Christ
is lovely in eyes and lovely in limbs not his,
eyes and limbs pierced in quiet places,
under the hammer, where no one hears,
and the choice is made when no one notices.

III: JEUX D'ESPRIT

Nowadays all we can tell you is
this:
what we are *not*, what we do *not*
want.

> – Eugenio Montale,
> *Cuttlefish Bones*

Economics in Aldeburgh

Fundamentally, there are only two
ways of co-ordinating the
economic activities of millions.
One is central direction involving
the use of coercion – the technique
of the army and the modern
totalitarian state. The other is
voluntary cooperation of
individuals – the technique of the
market place.

– Milton Friedman

Living here, between a nuclear station,
and a sea-wall tides are slowly battering down,
everything's privilege, peace, stagflation.
Easy to be content with this little town –
content! No sign in that of economic health:
one ought to be chasing utilities and wealth.

Economists know that man's a maximiser,
his aim to maximise both wealth and pleasure.
War's fun, utility, and makes us wiser.
To give's not human. Enough's no treasure.
Freed man has learned the way to be humane:
The market maketh man and makes him sane.

The myth of a mixed economy's evasion.
The market has no need of public pelf.
Coercion's inessential to civilisation.
The market's free: you're free to sell yourself,
be sold, or unemployed: it's funny
how people hate to work but do love money.

A maxi-miser: man's a mini-miser in this locale –
miser of his uneasy, guilty luck.
The only defence he needs is against the real:

a sea wall, death, failed life, his love unstuck:
no money for these, unlike the planes and tanks
he buys to fight the reds or please the banks.

Ancient Walls

The ancient walls with their patient lichens
are filling the graveyard with patience.

The poppy has chosen this little grave,
and the rhus spreads red leaves.

The horse-chestnut drops little polished
knobs: new brown shoes.

The old man's face and the girl's face
make the avenue of yews a frame.

In the Sunday distance a towering
hazy-morning steel crane is abandoned.

Dives comes out with the congregation,
and a wino Lazarus asks, Any change?

The Slow Motion of Trees

Hawthorn-soldiers
in their diminishing rank –

is it their spine or mine
crooked by the prevailing wind?

Or those slow
chestnut-meditations on roots,

is it their wine or mine
draining and winding down?

And oaks gesticulating
blindly in no wind,

is it the acorn in the heart
that makes their growing
a fisty centuries-long grind?

The Opera Lovers

In Act One
the opera lovers
discover each other:
history stops;
eternity begins.

In Act Two
the lovers discover
how the earth spins
on history's sins.

In Act Three
history wins
and the lovers discover
how history stops
and the overture begins.

Mathematics

Mathematics could always induce
an incalculable window-gazing curl
of glazed looking – to blush from, if questioned,
like caught red-handed with a girl.

And still a guest can glaze him through the glass
to tug with starlings, tails in air,
officious for something delicious
they're nippy for down there,

or to feel the wintery feeling
of the double-boled bow-legged pear,
or the down-in-the-roots horse-chestnut,
or the holly tasting the Christmas air.

Holy Leisure

Make all your life a holy leisure

– St Francis

His voice is the cat-purr
of a man trapped in a cell,
planning his escape.
He's a gambler: in the funny
business of buying and selling money.

Drink is out: his stomach says no.
His wife's hoping to make enough bread
or call it dough
to let the butterflies out of his stomach
and play round his boat instead.

She's frightened of him waltzing off
with the perfumed lady with
the leisurely alternative life.
Death frightens him
even more than his wife.

He pads stealthy, soft-pawed,
as if cased by MI5
or hoods on contract:
a cat that's been watching
thrushes all day, hunchbacked,

and now feels ogled itself
as, squeezed by jungle,
in obscure need of pardon,
it picks its way
out of the garden.

The Longest Sentences

Pour dire les plus longues phrases,
Elle n'a pas besoin de mots.

        – Baudelaire, 'Le Chat'

In these dreams he's often teaching students
who don't want to come. They stroll in late,
won't settle down, titter, knit. He gets in, oh,
about five minutes of the proper stuff before
they're packing bags and ready to go.

'In Blake's *Visions*,' he explains, 'a virgin's sweetly
concupiscent, and sets off to find her lover, but
meets a cynic on the way, who rapes her by surprise.
Now here's a short story or novella,
but Blake makes his characters philosophize.

'Conrad speaks of "justification": make
your characters philosophize to taste,
so long as you plot a plausible premise
for your people to analyse their case.'
The class is drifting off in fantasies.

And then, to his hot shame, he's weeping tears.
'Teaching's a vocation,' he breaks and cries.
'You've taken the joy away.' They shake their curls, they
rush to him in gusts of kind dismay.
They warm to his self-pity. They're girls.

At the Seminar

In the seminar room the sun
is shining on the desk more than anyone
can feel or say.

Isn't there, he wonders, some way
to get his students to see
how displacing a shine can be?

Even the poem's about
how signifiers can throw out
all capacity to see and be.

Instead of all this pother
if only we could just gently get together
washing and massaging each other.

Egg on a Mantelpiece

Some parchment-skinned Chinese
painted these boats, this pagoda,
this high peak and these
incomprehensible characters
for a pittance
on this eggshell.

In bad taste as well.
So thin a duster could break it,
and given in love,
it's lasted for years.

All history resides
on a souvenir
from a hen's insides.

Hard

It's hard to forgive the trivial things,
the dirt, the incompetence, the self-neglect
and the shambling practices.

It's difficult to forgive the smells,
the tobacco, the drink, the violence,
the need to be in control:

the desire to be top bully in a little world.
It's difficult to forgive them your snobbery.
It's difficult to need so much forgiveness,

to be ready for a heaven where there are
mothers and fathers and uncles and children.

Waiting in Wet

The metal bird appears to be watching me.
The old dog is bored by the puppy's attentions.
An ear-nibbling only makes him
sad, with the sadness of dogs.

The irritating persistence of rain hums,
and clouds curl round the would-be sunny ridges;
a cock crows occasionally, unconvincedly,
round the hill: boredom's current images.

The flies must know the sun will be coming out,
for they're coming out themselves. Or is it lunchtime,
and do they know? A carhorn crows down the valley,
with a frustrated wailing.

After a thousand miles, one rests
in a kind of driver's convalescence. The map's lost,
I've no watch, and action is stopped
by the steady downpour. I yawn and cannot read.

Even the olives are depressed.
The rain they're used to they don't need.
Into their second century, they're not going to
accept a drenching without a droop.

Into the second chapter I droop
but don't complain. In England there's a drought.
At least the wine here brings no headache.
Later I wake without a headache to the rain.

By the Lake

A red pinebole glows like sunset
and I hug my arms around it.

A roach's eye glows in the lake:
a ruby. It sees my eye;
we watch each other.

Past the adder's nest
I met an elk:
we stared; he strolled away.

Two hares come boxing
on hind legs through the forest.
They see me and panic.

One part of my mind's a hare.
It's been dominating the rat.
Now the rat's eating the brain of the hare.

Holes

There's a hole in the atom, between
electron and neutron, as distant
as Lords from Sydney.

I hoard gold inside me, with
sulphur, silver, the rest,
and holes leak my insides out.

My head's a hole in space
with no splash; a neutrino
quarks two holes in me at once.

There's a hole where someone was:
a hole in a mirror:
itself a hole in the wall.

Grief makes holes in a face
and so does laughter. The womb's
a hole, the soul's a hole,

and Felicity's the name of a cat
going through a hole
just wide enough for her whiskers.

Anyway, it isn't Somatic

It's impossible to be a conformist
unless I stupefy myself with smoke.
        As soon as I give up smoking
        I get notions:

like, why not try some new ideas?
But liberty, of course, means
        a rather frightening
        polymorphous kind of freedom.

Byron, for example, why did he escape to Greece
instead of creating a society
        for the protection
        of good ideas?

And what about the long overdue Leisure Party?
Even with planned obsolescence, meat mountains,
        wine lakes, and
        subsidised idle acres,

can we make buying and selling money
the main business till the big bang
        reverses and contracts
        towards the crunch?

Must we admit we're snuffing production
to buck up the rationing system?
        Can we really go on generating money
        as our main product?

The fear rises that Bingo would be
more harmless than banking, insurance
        and the bourse, even though
        computer games are fun.

As the smoke clears from my cortex,
I start to visualise a new
        eighteenth-century aristocracy,
        for us all.

The cabinet appears on the media
and tells everyone that toil
        and money are
        poisoning output.

Their wish to conceal that superabundance
slashes prices and prosperity
        is bad for business
        has foundered.

Be satisfied with free cars, they say,
free food, free televisions, free
        washing machines and
        toiling automatons.

A simulation shows a man
feeding his old car into the recycler,
        selecting a new one
        and driving off.

He puts all his garbage
into an orifice under the sink
        where it goes
        straight to the infrastructure.

The post office closes down
and is replaced by fax.
        Illusion closes down
        and is replaced by facts.

We see a call-up of the eighteen-year-olds
for two years' toil. At twenty
        they walk free to face
        the terrors of self-realisation.

But how will we escape with no wars?
Will we feel safe with sport,
          art, opera, science,
          social work, or yoga?

Shall we have to organise controlled
football violence? Or can we too live
          as aristocrats lived,
          content with inherited handouts:

killing birds, breeding horses,
training dogs, playing polo,
          giving huge gourmet picnics,
          parties and balls? –

devoting days and nights
to love affairs? Of course,
          those who love power
          can govern the country.

But can *we* live without fake problems,
or seek escape up mountains,
          or race aeroplanes
          upside down?

We may be here for millenia!
Can we spend them growing
          the sidewhiskers
          of the nineteenth century?

I must fill the void with smoke,
or vested interests preventing the future
          will seem a family
          of delinquent primates –

and they're my fellow-men!
So I'm waiting for some scientist
          to prove that smoking
          isn't caused by cancer.

Notes on Lao Tzu

After the long silence with no one listening words split the
                                        beginning from the end.

Told he was dying, he said, 'Ah well, that's life'.
However much he breathed, there was still more air.
Turning from the mirror, he was someone else.
He praised the dead, for no one envied them.
The tree let go its leaf without relief.

Without means meaningless, without end he was endless.
He evaporated like water and fell like water.
Too much was more than enough.
He led from below and got a head.
The hole in the clay made him a pot.

If he went into the hole in the ground he'd never fear
                                        death again.
He suspected a merger but in the end the company
                                        just kept going.
The hidden was making secret investments.
His heart ached – there was so little at stake.
Too much light was making him blind.

He knew his mother's wishes were not his mother's.
His only hope was to escape from her advice.
When his father went to gaol he found he loved him.
A fool among fools, his only hope was to obey the rules.
Crossing the ice his step was precise.

His anxiety when he was not succeeding was only
                    exceeded by his anxiety when he was.
Not at home even at home, he became less at home.
His apologies were inexcusable.
He tried to admire himself and failed.
Everything was so strange he walked along listening.

He travelled effortlessly under gravity.
His temptation was to reject the easy way.
When he meant what he said he didn't know what he was
saying.
Like the drunk in the street, he slept with his head away
from his feet.
He never got too far in advance of the cookhouse.

Waste was bad, even of people.
He made a killing and it felt like a funeral.
Not knowing he needed saving he couldn't save anyone.
The ruler of the world had always ended up in a bunker
with a woman and a dog.
History was the history of discontent.

It wasn't easy to leave people alone.
Giving the people bread made government a piece of cake.
When the government was bad the people were happy.
By their prime ministers they knew them.
A good leader was invisible as the retina.

Although there was enough to go round it didn't go round.
The fat country had a thin country inside.
Reading the paper he knew more than he could
understand.
The people were divided up among the loaves and fishes.
In his dream he remembered what he hadn't noticed.

If he'd invented air we'd all be gasping at the price.
Asked to choose between his big toe and fame he chose his
toe.
It was too easy to find a reason for everything.
To make an omelette he'd needed to cook sensitively.
He didn't want to hurt the con-man's feelings by noticing.

But his problems acquired confidence.
He couldn't spot the beginnings before they happened.
The deepest vacuum was the biggest draw.
The best of the bargain was the worst.
Goodness was badly paid.

Flowery words yielded to seeds.
In the Old Folks' Home people were growing.
The man with the smile was a crippled roadsweeper.
Comfort was an oyster with no pearl.
The old soldier took his time.

The air was more secure than the balloon.
His absence was more than a presence.
What happened inside him happened outside.
Those doing the same thing weren't doing the same thing.
The starter was a loser.

Ill-bred, he tried to breed the well-bred.
There were more ways of eating than with a knife and
                                                     fork.
Since he'd never die, he wouldn't multiply.
The generous host wasn't respected the most.
The truth made him laugh.

But he said so little they thought 'We did this ourselves'.
The sea curtseyed, retreated and then swallowed a church.
It was hard to decide about death without knowing what it
                                                   was.
Even if he'd known the map he'd have lost the way.
Unlike the wind, when he started blowing he had to go on.

The Santa Sophia of Air

The great forward movements of
the Renaissance all derive their
vigour, their emotional impulse,
from looking backward.

– Frances A. Yates, *Giordano Bruno*
and the Hermetic Tradition, 1964

In the lantern of the upper air, sun
breeds a tropic. The conservatory
of gases turns the warming on.

The first big bang was silent: the ring
of quiet clogged into sounds we hear:
Alpha heard a crystal Omega sing.

Justinian thought he'd invented the new:
four arches, a floating dome of let-in lights.
'Solomon,' he said, 'I've triumphed over you.'

But Hebrew prophecy, Roman and Eastern design
moulded the spandrels, the marbles, the glass mosaics:
lacy predictions of the Florentine.

We too anticipate the past: night
is our hemisphere, but domes diagram
half only of our balloon of light.

The cold blue radiations of space
make an architecture of refraction:
fake-solid spectra of place and race.

Aping faces gape from the gas and dust.
They mop and mow and crunch the forest mast.
A connoisseur keeps the best wine till the last.

Author's Note

'Two-hundred-mile-an-hour Winds': I read in *The National Geographic Magazine* about two people and a donkey who were lifted thousands of feet in the air by a tornado, stripped and dropped, shocked but alive, miles away. This seemed to me too typical a human experience – at least at the psychological level – to be overlooked.

It's obvious there are many direct allusions in 'The Wild Swans at Aldeburgh' and 'Remembering Adlestrop', but I suppose the point had better be explicit. There are, of course, other minor allusions in the book.

I tried to keep as close as possible to Montale (1896–1981) in 'Unaccompanied Voices' (1939) but occasionally had to rearrange syntax and guess or choose about obscure or ambiguous passages; so I called the work an 'imitation'. Any version of Horace is necessarily an 'imitation', but there is, of course, a long and healthy tradition of imitating him. Why imitate? As someone said, all art is a collaboration.

Some time after I'd written item 2 of 'Notes on Lao Tzu' I came across this in Alan Ross's review of Brian Adams's *Such is Life: A Biography of Sidney Nolan*:
> 'Such is life' were, reputedly, the last words to be uttered by Ned Kelly, the Australian bushranger, before he was hanged.

I find such synchronicities intriguing, though probably meaningless. The same week I came down in the middle of the night, unable to sleep, went straight to Robert Graves's *Collected Poems* and opened it at a poem I didn't remember having read before – beginning 'Not to sleep all the night long, for pure joy . . .'

In 'Keith Vaughan's Last Journal' I've kept as close as I could to Vaughan's own words and images. The selection and arrangement – and therefore the interpretation – are of course mine. Suffering Vaughan's scarifying last words, I was most moved by God's efforts to reach Vaughan through what he loved, cared for and understood.

PW 1/02/5/alun